Mooch Forever

Gilles Gauthier

Illustrations by Pierre-André Derome

Translated by Sarah Cummins

D1262249

Formac Publishing Limited
Halifax, Nova Scotia
1995

Originally published as Ma Babouche pour toujours

Copyright © 1990 la courte échelle

Translation copyright © 1995 by Formac Publishing Limited

Canadian Cataloguing in Publication Data

Gauthier, Gilles, 1943-

[Ma Babouche pour toujours. English]

Mooch Forever

(First Novel Series)

Translation of: Ma Babouche pour toujours.

ISBN 0-88780-308-3 (paper)
ISBN 0-88780-309-1 (board)

I. Derome, Pierre-André, 1952- II. Title. III. Title: Ma Babouche pour toujours, English. IV. Series.

PS8563.A858M313 1995   jc843'.54   C95-950089-8
PZ7.G3Mo 1995

Formac Publishing Limited
5502 Atlantic Street
Halifax, N.S. B3H 1G4

Printed and bound in Canada

Table of contents

1
An empty place in my heart

"Veterinarians! What are they good for? Those shots were useless. Vets pretend to take care of your animals, then they let them die!

"Afterwards they tell you any old garbage. 'Your dog died of old age. When an animal gets to a certain age, there's nothing anyone can do.'

"That vet was a liar, Mom. Nine years old is too young for anyone to die! Even a dog. Nobody dies at the age of nine!

"Yes, I know, her paws had been giving her trouble. But did

you ever hear of anyone dying from sore paws? If you're having trouble with your paws, you get them treated!"

"Carl, the vet explained it all to you. Mooch's heart gave out."

"Mooch's heart was better than any vet's heart! I'll never believe her heart gave out. She died because that ignorant vet poisoned her with his horrible medicine.

"All Mooch wanted was to live quietly with us, for two or three more years. But then the vet had to stick his nose in, and now I'm all alone."

"Calm down, Carl. Try to calm down. You know very well that Dr. Norman did everything he could, but Mooch—"

"I know, she was too old! That must be the tenth time you've said that! And I telling you that Dr. Norman is a liar. There was no reason for Mooch to die!"

"Mooch was very sick."

"I never heard her complain."

"Her paws hurt so much she spent the whole day licking them. You saw her."

"All dogs lick their paws. They're not like pigs! They try to keep clean!"

"She had a lot of trouble breathing, too."

"She still wanted to go on living, even if her paws were wrecked, even if she limped a little."

"She was getting skinnier every day."

"She would have got stronger again, if she had had the time. Mooch was never a quitter. If your brilliant doctor hadn't butted in, Mooch would never have left me!"

2
Hurting

Nothing seems to interest me, ever since Mooch died. Nothing at all.

School is a disaster. I wasn't that fond of school to begin with. Now I think it stinks.

I don't want to have anything to do with anyone. I don't care if I flunk!

I wish I could just give up the whole thing.

And I wish Gary would just go away, him and his stupid little dog.

DUMPLING! Is that name dorky enough for you?

And the worst of it is, the name fits the dog perfectly.

Gary's dad probably got him really cheap.

I know that when you've just come out of prison you don't

have a lot of money, but still, I think he might have tried a little harder.

Ever since Mooch died, Gary is always asking me to go play at his house. It's no use. I don't feel like playing.

And anyway, I can't stand his stupid Dumpling!

I would rather think about Mooch.

Most of the time when I think about her, I feel all broken up inside. My eyes fill with tears.

And then gradually I calm down. Sometimes I put my head down on my desk at school, and I can even laugh to myself, when I think of the crazy things my dog used to do.

I can still see her, late at night, refusing to go outside to do her

business. Just because it's rain-
ing and Miss Mooch doesn't
want to get her paws wet on the
grass.

I can see her tiptoeing around,
trying to skip between the rain-
drops, like a ballet dancer.

I remember her when Mom
and I used to come back from

the grocery store. What a lot of
help she was!

As soon as she saw us with the
grocery bags full to the brim,

she'd stick like glue, getting un-
derfoot every step of the way
home. Right into the kitchen!

Then she'd stick her nose in the bags to see what we had bought. And she'd poke her head into the fridge as we put the meat away, hoping to get a little present.

I really wish she would come back. I was so happy with Mooch.

How come she had to die?

How come it was Mooch who died? Like Dad.

How come it wasn't a stupid little dog like Dumpling that died instead?

3
Afraid

Mom doesn't know what to do with me. I'm always sad and I've lost my appetite. I know that Mom is unhappy.

Every so often she tries to talk to me, but I won't listen. I already know what she's going to say.

Anyway, she can't give me the one and only thing I want—my dog.

I want Mooch, with her weird scruffy fur that shed everywhere. Mooch, with her warm, soft fur.

When I go to bed at night, it

seems almost as if Mooch is there with me, curled up at my feet, looking like a German shepherd who has been through the wars, with her big, glassy eyes.

Without her, the house is empty, deserted.

I miss Mooch. I love her so much.

I love Mooch as much as I love Judy, my mom. I do. It sounds funny, but it's true.

Anyway, I don't believe that there is that much difference between animals and humans.

Mooch could talk to me. She talked with her eyes and ears and her body. Sometimes when she started barking, she sounded like she was speaking in sentences. I understood everything she was telling me.

I love Mooch as much as I love Mom. And as much as I loved Dad, when he was alive.

But now I'm afraid. First Dad. Now Mooch. I'm afraid

that there is another name on the list.

I don't want to be left all alone in the world. Without Mom.

4
Gary's surprise

This morning I got quite a surprise. First Gary came over with Dumpling.

As soon as I laid eyes on them, I got mad. I yelled at him to go back home and take his awful dog with him. But Gary stayed calm and said he absolutely had to talk to me.

Judy came and told me to let them in, at least for a few minutes. Just long enough to hear what Gary had to say.

That's when I got the surprise of my life. Gary offered to give me his dog. He said that he had

thought it over very carefully and he was certain that I needed a dog more than he did.

He said he knew Dumpling wasn't an intelligent dog like Mooch, but with enough time I could probably teach him a few things. He insisted that I take Dumpling.

I didn't know what to think. Two minutes earlier, I couldn't stand Dumpling, even though I'd never seen him up close. Now I wasn't so sure.

Judy asked Gary if his dad knew about this offer. He said that they had talked it over and his dad had agreed.

Dumpling stood there in front of me, wide-eyed, wagging his tail, as if he was waiting for my verdict.

Gary said that since Dumpling was still a young dog, he would have fewer problems getting used to a new master. And

since I had so much experience with dogs ...

I was stunned. I didn't know what to think, with that funny little fuzzy dog looking at me out of the corner of his eye.

Seeing my indecision, Gary finally opened the door and said, "Take some time to think it over. I'll leave Dumpling here

overnight, so you get a good idea of what he's like. I'll stop by again tomorrow."

And before I could react, Gary ran out. Dumpling dashed to the door to follow his master.

I was tempted to open the door and let Dumpling out. But I just didn't make a move. But I don't know why, I just didn't make a move.

After a minute or two, Dumpling stopped yapping and sat down in front of the door, pricking up his ears at the slightest noise. Then he turned and looked straight into my eyes.

All of a sudden he began to seem less stupid.

Dumpling is a funny little dog. He definitely has nothing in common with Mooch.

But he does have an intelligent look about him.

5
My dog for a day

Dumpling is quite the fellow! He's a real clown!

First of all, Sir Dumpling will drink only milk. Judy and I found that out pretty quick. He splashes so much milk all over

his chin that he winds up looking like Santa Claus.

When it comes to food, he's
no champion either. He has
trouble eating the dry dog food
we bought him. He practically
needs a nutcracker before he
can chew it.

And he's so little he can
hardly climb up onto my bed.
Already he's made two big
holes in the bedspread trying to

claw his way up like a jungle cat.

Speaking of cats, I know now that Dumpling has at least one thing in common with Mooch. He is just as terrified of the neighbours' tomcat called Smoky as Mooch was.

When he spotted Smoky on the street yesterday, he started to

shake and he came and hid be-
hind me. Just like Mooch.

There is one other thing I've
noticed about Dumpling. He has
never once for a single second
stopped thinking about Gary,
ever since he came.

Even when he seems to be
having fun, after a little while
he'll go and look out the door, as

if he's checking to see if Gary is coming.

Dogs are very faithful. Much more than Gary thinks. A dog isn't a toy that can belong to you one day and to someone else the next. Even if you have a good reason.

Dumpling is already very attached to Gary. I can see that. I can feel it.

Dumpling is not as silly as I thought. I could probably make something out of him over the long term. But he doesn't belong here.

He belongs with Gary, the greatest friend I've ever had.

Except for Mooch, of course.

6
Dog-sharing

It's weird what happened when Gary came back to find out what I had decided.

Instead of speaking, I ran straight to him and gave him a big hug. Just like that, without even thinking about it ahead of time.

I know how much Dumpling means to Gary. So I hugged him to show him that I appreciated what he had tried to do for me.

We both started crying. For me that's not unusual. I cry all the time. But this was the first

time I had ever seen Gary cry.

After we calmed down a bit, I told Gary straight out what I thought. Dumpling is his dog, and there is no way he can give Dumpling to me, but I would be willing to help him train his dog.

Gary said that he would love

to have the full benefit of my experience. He wants me to teach Dumpling everything I can. We even started right then and there.

I had shown Mooch how to count to two. I used cookies to do it. If she barked once, I gave her one cookie. If she barked twice in a row, I gave her two cookies.

She never managed to count up to three. And it wasn't from lack of trying on my part. I fed her tons of cookies, but it was no use.

She must have had some kind of block with the number three. A learning disability, as they say at school.

Judy told me that I had lot of problems with the number three, too. When I was three years old, I would always hold up two fingers when people asked me how old I was. Mooch was sort of like me.

Gary and I thought we would try to teach Dumpling early. He's young, so he should be able to learn quickly.

That's what we thought BEFORE we used up two entire boxes of chocolate-chip cookies. Dumpling was still barking any old way and lying there with his stomach swollen like a soccer ball.

7
Mooch, Dad, Judy, and Me

I don't know how it is that my mom can always tell what I'm thinking. It happened again yesterday while we were looking at some slides.

We were looking at a slide of Dad holding baby Mooch in his arms. But Judy knew I was thinking about her, and what would happen to me if she were to disappear too.

We talked for a long time. About life and death.

Judy told me that Mooch was old and sick. She had given us everything she could, and then she was gone.

Judy said she knew it was hard for me to see the vet carrying Mooch's body away, after I had said my last goodbyes to her. But she made me understand that the vet hadn't taken away the most important part.

We had been happy together with Mooch for many years. Nobody could take that time away from us. Mooch would always be a big piece of happiness in our hearts. Forever.

I felt that it was harder for Judy to explain about Dad.

She told me that life is a bit like a play, in the theatre. Some of the actors are on stage for a long time, others not so long. But every one has a part to play, and every part is an important one.

Everyone has to discover what part to play and play it as best he can. So that everybody's life will be as happy as it can be.

Mooch and Dad played their parts. Judy said that she and Dad had been very, very happy together. And Dad loved me very much.

She said she was proud of me.
She said that I have played my

part very well so far. With her, and with Mooch and Dad.

And she told me she had no intention of leaving me all alone on the stage of life.

Judy and I talked together for a long time. She helped me a lot. We talked and laughed together.

We laughed about when we went to the Island, and Mooch would chase seagulls for hours on end. Those seagulls had the nerve to try and land on HER beach!

We laughed when we remembered how Mooch got sick after eating too much "seafood"— old, dried-out lobster shells she found.

And poor Mooch, who couldn't blow out the candles on her birthday cake.

Good old Mooch, our four-legged dishwasher, always willing to clean up everybody's plates after meals.

Crazy Mooch, who always thought she'd spied another dog every time she looked in the mirror.

The time Mooch was disguised as a hockey player for Hallowe'en.

We cried together too, talking about Mooch and thinking about Dad.

8
The Book of Mooch

Today I have two great pieces of news.

First, Judy told me about our summer holidays. Guess where we're going?

Back to the Island!

But that's not all. Do you know who's coming with us? You'll never guess!

Gary! And Dumpling! We're all going to the Island together.

I haven't slept a wink since Judy told me. I can't wait until school is over. I wish I could just skip some days. Or put a motor on the earth so that it would turn faster.

Gary has never been to the Island. I can't wait to show him

all the favourite hiding places Mooch and I had found, in the red rock caves beside the sea. Dumpling is bound to get lost.

And the other good news?

I have decided to write a book during our summer vacation. A

real book, like the books in the libraries and bookstores.

But not just any old book. Not a boring book, or a baby book.

A book about MOOCH!

I will tell the story of Mooch. About our life together, all the crazy things we did.

It will be funny in parts and pretty sad in other parts.

But especially, it's going to be a true story. It will tell about a real nine-year-old kid, me, and a real nine-year-old dog, Mooch.

When Mooch died, I wanted to have her stuffed, but Judy said I couldn't. Actually, she was right to say no. Stuffed animals are ugly. It's like they're frozen on the spot.

With my book, everybody will have a much better idea of

what Mooch was really like. It'll be like giving her a second chance at life.

I haven't decided on a title for my book yet, but Mooch's name should be in the title. She's the star of the book, after all.

But I think I already know how I will begin.

Imagine Mooch lying on the living-room rug. She's asleep

and dreaming, as she often was. I'm sitting beside her and describing what I see.

The first sentence of my book should go something like this:

Look! Mooch is dreaming again.

It will be just as if Mooch is still alive.

That's what I want most of all.

Look for these First Novels!
Collect the entire series!

About Maddie
Maddie in Danger
Maddie Goes to Paris
Maddie Wants Music
That's Enough, Maddie
Maddie in Goal

About Mooch
Mooch Forever
Hang On, Mooch
Mooch Gets Jealous
Mooch and Me

About Arthur
Arthur's Problem Puppy
Arthur's Dad
Arthur Throws a Tantrum

About the Swank twins
The Swank Prank
Swank Talk

About Mikey Mite
Mikey Mite Goes to School
Mikey Mite's Big Problem

About the Loonies
Loonie Summer
The Loonies Arrive

And meet Fred and Raphael!
Fred's Dream Cat
Video Rivals

And more to come!

For more information about these and other fine books for young readers contact

Formac Publishing Company Limited
5502 Atlantic Street
Halifax, Nova Scotia B3H 1G4
(902) 421-7022 Fax (902) 425-0166